The Happy Baker

C.A. Nobens

Carolrhoda Books · Minneapolis, Minnesota

Copyright © 1979 by CAROLRHODA BOOKS, INC.

All rights reserved. International copyright secured. Manufactured in the United States of America. Published simultaneously in Canada by J. M. Dent & Sons (Canada) Ltd., Don Mills, Ontario.

LIBRARY OF CONGRESS CATALOGING IN PUBLICATION DATA

Nobens, C. A.
The happy baker.

(On my own books)
SUMMARY: Although Joseph loves his little town, his little bakery, his little house, and his little pets, he longs to see the rest of the big world.

[1. Bakers and bakeries—Fiction. 2. Bread—Fiction] I. Title.

PZ7.N664Hap   [E]   79-88198
ISBN 0-87614-109-2 lib. bgd.

1   2   3   4   5   6   7   8   9   10   85   84   83   82   81   80   79

to Curtis
who washed the dishes for a whole month
while I painted these pictures

Once there was a very happy baker.
His name was Joseph.

He lived in two tiny cozy rooms
above his tiny little bakery
in a tiny little town.
Every morning Joseph got up
before the sun.

He went down to his bakery.

And he put out his sign.

Here is what it said.

And that was quite true,

for Joseph was the only baker in town.

Then Joseph put on his apron.

And he put on his baker's hat.

And he went to work baking bread.

Wonderful smells came from his ovens.

They floated out the door
and down the street.
And everybody in town
came to buy Joseph's bread.

Joseph lived with three good friends —
a cat named Alice,
and a mouse named Henry,
and a bird named Phyllis.
Unlike many cats and mice and birds,
Alice and Henry and Phyllis
got along very well together.
Maybe that was because
they always had lots to eat.
Every night Joseph climbed the stairs
from his bakery to his two cozy rooms
and made a fine meal for them.
Bread and a big bowl of milk for Alice.
Bread crusts and cheese for Henry.
And bread crumbs for Phyllis.

11

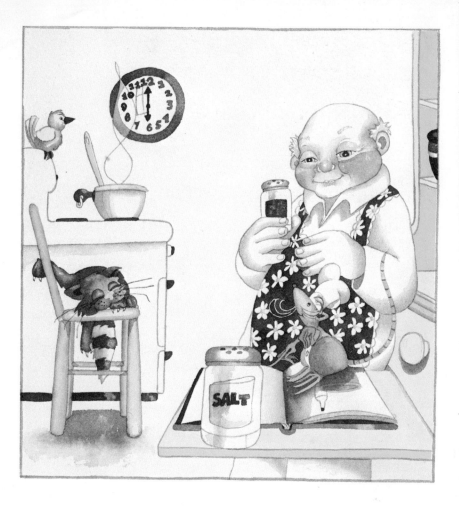

Then Joseph made his own supper.

You guessed it.

Bread with lots of butter.

Sometimes he had a little hot soup too.

And for dessert?

Bread pudding, of course.

With raisins.

All in all, Joseph was very happy

with his life.

And so were Alice and Henry and Phyllis.

But there was one thing
that sometimes made him feel
a little bit sad.
Joseph wanted to see the wide world.

Every once in a while
he would think about great castles
in far away places.

"I know this house is very cozy,"
he would say then.
"But it is so tiny."

Sometimes he would sip his tea
and think about giant bakeries
in big cities.
"I know I am a lucky man
to have such a fine little bakery,"
he would say then.
"But it is so very small."

17

One day Joseph made up his mind.

"I will do it," he said. "Why not?"

That week he baked in the mornings.

And he baked in the afternoons.

And he baked in the nights.

By the end of the week
he had baked enough bread
to last the little town a long time.

Then he packed his suitcase.

He said good-bye to his many friends.

And he set off to see the world.

His first stop was France.

Joseph could not wait

to see the castles.

But he was hungry after his long trip.

"I will have a little lunch first,"

he said.

He asked for some bread and soup.

The soup looked very good.

"But this is not bread," said Joseph.

"This is how we make bread in France,"

said the waiter.

"It is far too long to be bread,"

said Joseph.

And he did not eat it.

He did eat the soup.

It was very very good.

So Joseph wrote down how to make it.

And then he saw some castles.

His next stop was Russia.

"Here I will get some bread,"
said Joseph.

And he asked for a whole loaf of bread
and a bowl of soup.

"But this is not bread," he said.

"This is how we make bread in Russia,"
said the waiter.

"It is far too dark to be bread,"
said Joseph.

And he did not eat it.

But the soup was yummy.

And Joseph wrote down how to make it.

In Israel Joseph tried again
to buy some bread.

"But this is not bread," he said.

"This is how we make bread in Israel
at Passover," said the waiter.

"It is only a big cracker,"
said Joseph.

"I will just have some soup."

This soup was the best yet.

So Joseph wrote down how to make it.

Maybe they will have bread in India,
Joseph thought.

But when he saw it, he said,

"Why, this can not be bread!"

"This is how we make bread in India,"
said the waiter.

"That can not be," said Joseph.

"This is nothing but a pancake
with a pocket.

Bring me some soup instead."

The soup was even better than the last.

So Joseph wrote down how to make it too.

Joseph's last stop was Mexico.

"Surely they will have bread here,"

he said.

He asked for bread and soup once more.

"What a mess!" he said

when he got the bread.

"Does no one know how to make bread?"
"This is how we make bread in Mexico,"
said the waiter.

"Yes," said Joseph.

"The soup is wonderful."

And he wrote down how to make it.

When Joseph got home,
he dropped his suitcase on the floor.
"Hello," he said to Alice and Henry
and Phyllis.

Then he ran right down to his bakery.

He put on his apron.

He put on his baker's cap.

And he baked the biggest loaf of bread
that anyone had ever seen.

He took the loaf of bread upstairs.

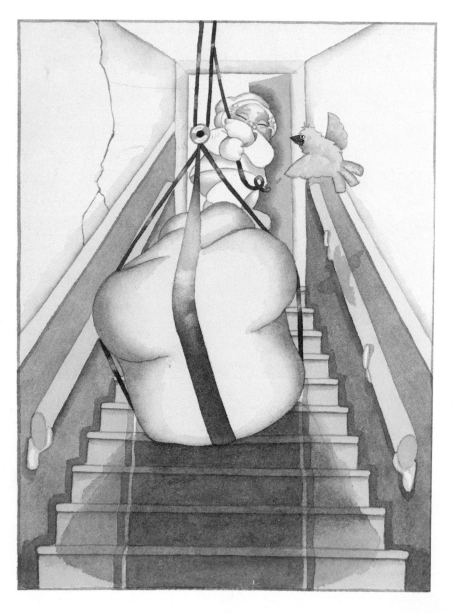

He gave Alice a small bowl of milk
and lots of fresh warm bread.
He gave Henry a little piece of cheese
and a huge slice of bread.
He gave Phyllis a giant bowl
of bread crumbs.

Then he sat down to eat with them.

"How good it feels to be home,"

he told them.

"This world is a very strange place.

Everybody in it makes wonderful soup.
But no one, no one in the whole world,
knows how to bake a loaf of bread.
No one, that is, but me."

The next day Joseph got up
before the sun.
But before he went down to his bakery,
before he put on his apron,
before he put on his baker's hat,
before he began to bake bread,
he made a brand new sign.
Here is what it said.

JOSEPH'S BAKERY AND SOUP SHOP
Travel east and travel west,
It's hard to tell which soup is best.
But if you want a slice of bread,
You must come to Joseph to be fed.

About the Author

C.A. Nobens grew up in northern Minnesota in a mining town named Hibbing. From there she moved around a bit and finally settled in Minneapolis. She graduated from the Minneapolis College of Art and Design. This is her first book.

Ms. Nobens spends her time drawing, writing, playing her piano (with three dead keys), upholstering furniture, hammering, sawing, gardening, cooking, making stained glass, and admiring freight trains, which she can see from the east windows of her 100-year-old house.